BY
SCOTT SONNEBORN

ILLUSTRATED BY
OMAR LOZANO

THE
NORTH POLICE

Meet the South Police

PICTURE WINDOW BOOKS
A CAPSTONE IMPRINT

The North Police is published by
Picture Window Books
a Capstone Imprint
1710 Roe Crest Drive
North Mankato, Minnesota 56003
www.capstonepub.com

Cataloging-in-Publication Data is available at the Library of Congress website.
ISBN: 978-1-4795-6486-6 (library binding)
ISBN: 978-1-4747-0031-3 (paperback)
ISBN: 978-1-4747-0036-8 (eBook)

Summary: One of the North Police's two greatest detectives is missing in action! The
South Police send their best officer to help crack the case. Unfortunately, the two
police stations are polar opposites!

Designer: Bob Lentz

Printed in China by Nordica
0415/CA21500537
042015   008843NORDF15

TABLE OF CONTENTS

CHAPTER 1
Missing! 7

CHAPTER 2
Honk! 13

CHAPTER 3
Rescue! 19

THE North POLICE

(NORTH POHL-eess)

The North Police are

the elves who solve crimes

at the North Pole.

These are their stories . . .

CHAPTER 1
Missing!

Detective Sprinkles of the
North Police rushed into the
chief's office.

"Detective Sugarplum is
gone, sir," cried Sprinkles.
"She's been missing all day!"

"That's because she's on vacation," replied the chief.

It was the day after Christmas. After working so hard on December 25, many elves had taken the day off.

"But what if there's

trouble?" Sprinkles worried.

"I've never solved a case

without a partner."

"You won't have to," said

the chief.

"The South Police sent one of their best officers to fill in," the chief explained.

The South Police officer waddled into the room.

"HONK!" he said.

Sprinkles leaned over to the chief. "Sir, that's a penguin," he whispered.

"Of course," said the chief. "That's who lives in the South Pole!"

"All the best officers in the South Police are penguins," the chief added.

"HONK!" agreed the penguin.

Suddenly, the police radio on the chief's desk squawked.

"There's trouble on the Christmas Town highway!" said a voice over the radio.

CHAPTER 2
Honk!

The Christmas Town

highway was jammed with

elves returning to the North

Pole after their day off.

The tow sleigh couldn't get

through to the trouble.

"No problem," said
Sprinkles. "I'll just use my
sleigh bell siren."

Sprinkles hit the button.

Nothing happened.

The sleigh bell siren was broken!

"Oh, no!" said Sprinkles.
"How will we get through all this traffic?"

"HONK!" said the penguin.

"Great idea!" said

Detective Sprinkles.

Sprinkles honked the

police sleigh's horn.

BEEP-BEEP! The traffic

moved out of the way.

Sprinkles and the South Police officer led the tow sleigh to the trouble.

It was Sugarplum! The ice road had cracked under her sleigh. She was stuck!

Suddenly, the ice broke!
Sugarplum's sleigh fell toward
the icy water below.

"Oh, no!" cried Sprinkles.
"If she hits the water, she'll be
frozen for sure!"

CHAPTER 3
Rescue!

Detective Sprinkles

jumped onto the tow sleigh.

He grabbed the tow rope.

Sprinkles threw the rope to

Sugarplum as she fell.

But he missed!

"HONK!" cried the South

Police Officer.

The penguin dove through

the air. He grabbed the rope

in his beak.

The penguin hooked the

rope onto Sugarplum's sleigh

as it dropped through the air.

Then the South Police

Officer splashed down into

the freezing water!

The rope caught the
sleigh just in time. Detective
Sugarplum was safe!

But what about the South
Police Officer?

"HONK!" said the penguin as he popped out of the water. He was okay, too!

"That water is much too cold for an elf," said Detective Sprinkles.

"But for a penguin,"
Sprinkles added, "I guess the
water is just right."

The tow sleigh pulled
Sugarplum and her sleigh
back onto the road.

"I knew you'd get here in time, Detective Sprinkles," Sugarplum said. "The North Police are always there when you need them."

"So are the South Police," added Sprinkles.

"HONK!" agreed the penguin.

The North Police smiled.

"Another case neatly wrapped!" they cheered.

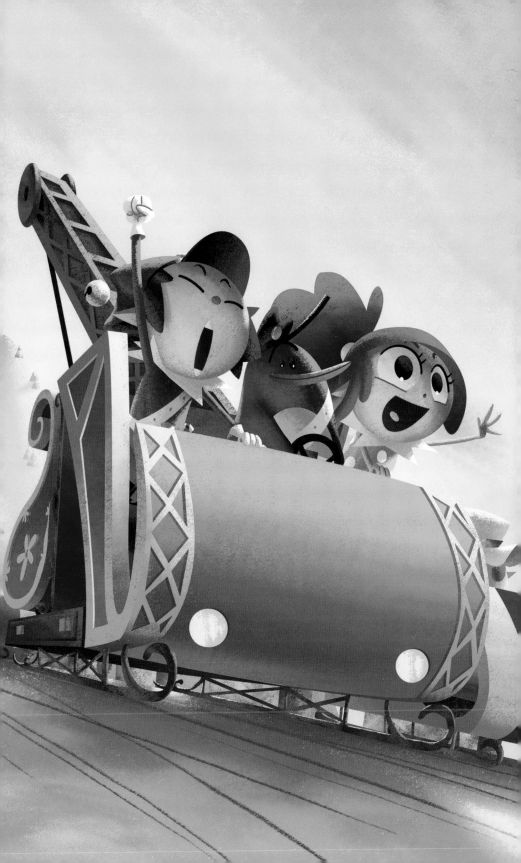

CASE SAVED!

6' 6"
6' 0"
5' 6"
5' 0"
4' 6"
4' 0"
3' 6"
3' 0"

CASE 002   NORTH POLICE
SOUTH POLICE
Penguin • Height 3'0" • Weight 50

GLOSSARY

detective (di-TEK-tiv) — one who investigates crimes

partner (PART-nuhr) — one of two people who do something together

siren (SYE-ruhn) — a device that makes a loud sound, which is used as a warning

sleigh (SLAY) — a sled usually pulled by horses or other animals

waddled (WAHD-uhld) — walked strangely, taking short steps and swaying from side to side

These are their stories . . .

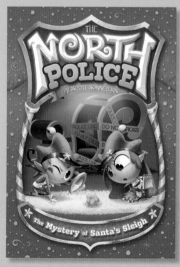

only from

Picture Window Books!

AUTHOR

Scott Sonneborn has written dozens of books, one circus (for Ringling Bros. Barnum & Bailey), and a bunch of TV shows. He's been nominated for one Emmy and spent three very cool years working at DC Comics. He lives in Los Angeles with his wife and their two sons.

ILLUSTRATOR

Omar Lozano lives in Monterrey, Mexico. He has always been crazy for illustration, constantly on the lookout for awesome things to draw. In his free time, he watches lots of movies, reads fantasy and sci-fi books, and draws! Omar has worked for Marvel, DC, IDW, Capstone, and more.